THE YELLOWEST
YELLOW LAB

The Yellowest Yellow Lab
Published by:
Three Bean Press, LLC
P.O. Box 15386
Boston, MA 02215 U.S.A.
Orders@threebeanpress.com • www.threebeanpress.com

Text copyright © 2005 by Seneca Clark and Sandy Giardi
Illustrations copyright © 2005 by Julie Decedue

Publishers Cataloging-in-Publication Data
Clark, Seneca Teal
Giardi, Sandy
The Yellowest Yellow Lab / by Seneca Clark and Sandy Giardi; illustrated by Julie Decedue.
p. cm.
Summary: A giant yellow lab is king of his pack, but he's afraid of everything.
ISBN 0-9767276-2-5
[1. Children—Fiction. 2. Dogs—Fiction. 3. Fears—Fiction.] I. Decedue, Julie, Ill.
II. Title.
LCCN 2005907921

Printed in the U.S.A.

Dedicated to:

Kaya-Whose wild, wagging tail makes everyone smile -S.C.

Cody-My favorite lounging buddy -J.D.

Gretzky-Decidedly yellow, but truly "the Great One" -S.G.

THE YELLOWEST YELLOW LAB IS THE BIGGEST ON HIS BLOCK.

ALL THE DOGS GAWK WHEN HE IS OUT FOR HIS WALK.

HE HAS A STRONG JAW AND A ROUND BARREL CHEST

AND A GROWL SO DEEP IT STANDS OUT FROM THE REST.

HE IS **KING** OF THE PACK,
WITH HIS BIG,
BLOCK-SHAPED HEAD,

YET THIS LAB HAS MORE FEARS
THAN THE DOGS HE HAS LED.

WITH A HEART OF PURE GOLD, HE'S
THE FRIENDLIEST FELLOW,

BUT, OH MY,
THAT SWEET DOG
IS DECIDEDLY

YELLOW!

AND EVEN
THOUGH THE LAB
IS AS BIG AS A

HOUSE,

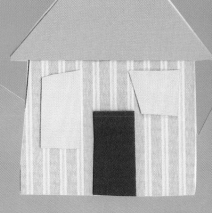

HE WILL FREEZE IN HIS TRACKS AT THE SIGHT OF A MOUSE.

MOUSE HOUSE

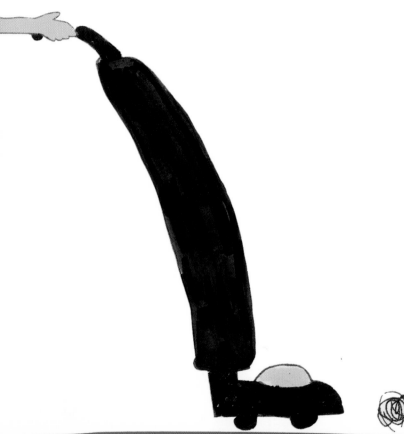

WHEN THE VACUUM CLEANER RUNS
WITH A LOUD, BEASTLY ROAR...

...IN A MATTER OF SECONDS
HE IS ON THE NEXT FLOOR.

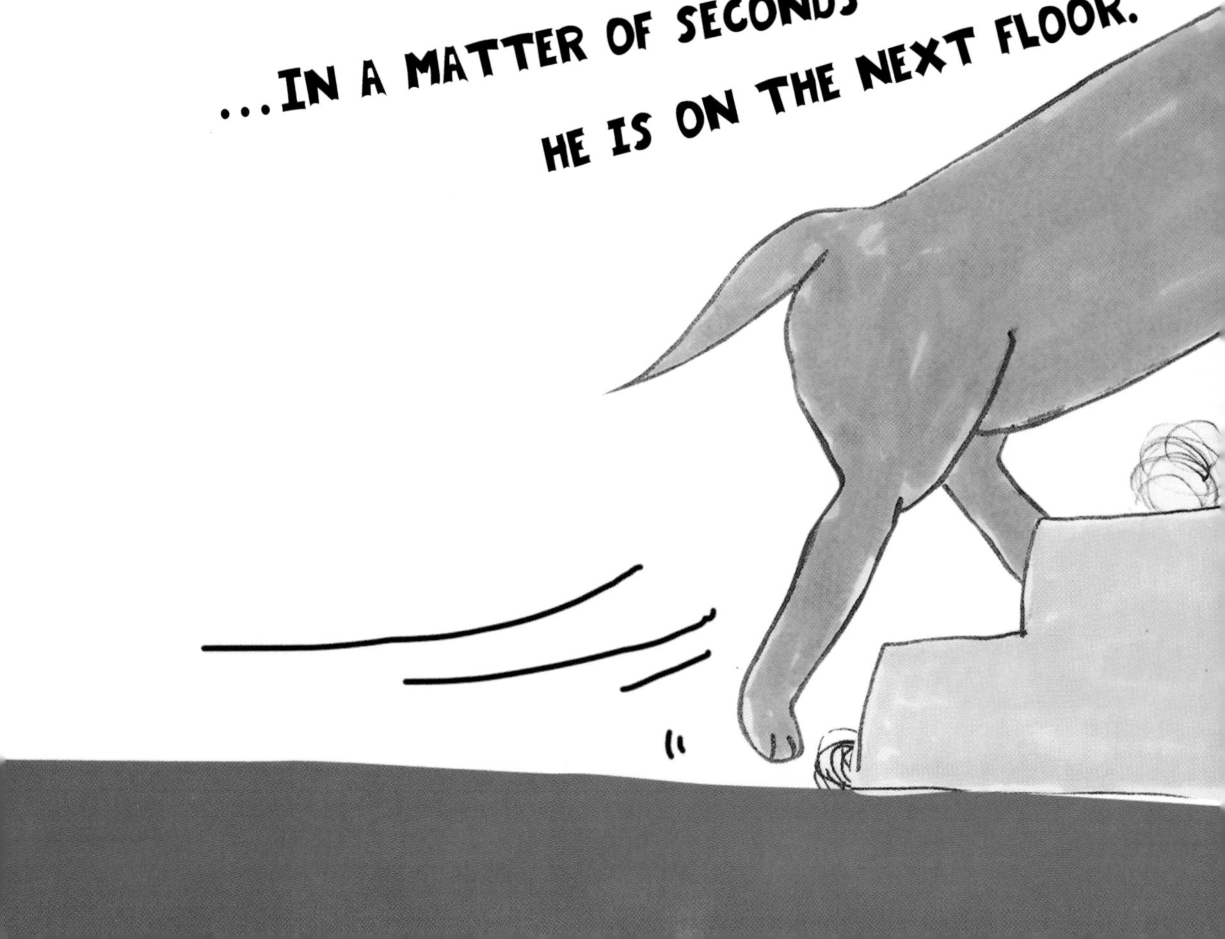

AND THOUGH
THE YELLOWEST
LAB LOVES TO
ROLL IN THE DIRT,

HE QUIVERS AT
BATH TIME

AS IF IT MIGHT HURT.

HE HIDES UNDER THE BED
AT THE FIRST CLAP OF

THUNDER.

"JUST WHY IS THIS DOG SO AFRAID?"

WE ALL WONDER.

THERE ARE
TWO FESTIVE
DAYS THAT

THE DOG JUST
CAN'T TAKE,

BUT THE REST
OF THE FAMILY

ADORES,
FOR PETE'S
SAKE!

AND ON HALLOWEEN, HE NEARLY JUMPS OUT OF HIS SKIN IF HE GLIMPSES A GHOST OR A GLOWING PUMPKIN.

THE YELLOW LAB'S A
SCAREDY-CAT,
IT'S DOGGONE TRUE.

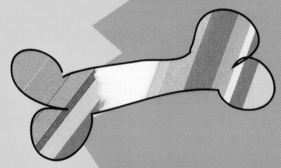

STILL, HE MAKES
YOU FEEL SAFE
WHEN HE SITS
NEXT TO YOU.

SAY YOU'RE HAVING A NIGHTMARE AND AWAKE WITH A **FRIGHT**,

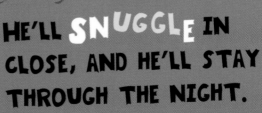

HE'LL **SNUGGLE** IN CLOSE, AND HE'LL STAY THROUGH THE NIGHT.

IF YOU'RE DOWN AND
YOU'RE BLUE, OR
YOU'VE HAD A BAD DAY,

THE WILD WAG OF
HIS TAIL MELTS YOUR
TROUBLES AWAY.

AND WHEN YOU'RE HOME BY YOURSELF, HE'LL STAY RIGHT AT YOUR HEELS,

BUT HE'S NEVER A NUISANCE— WELL, EXCEPT DURING MEALS.

LIKE THAT YELLOW YELLOW LAB, WE ALL
HAVE FEARS WE MUST FACE,

BUT WITH YOUR BEST FRIEND BESIDE
YOU, THE WORLD'S A HAPPIER PLACE!

THE END